DLEY

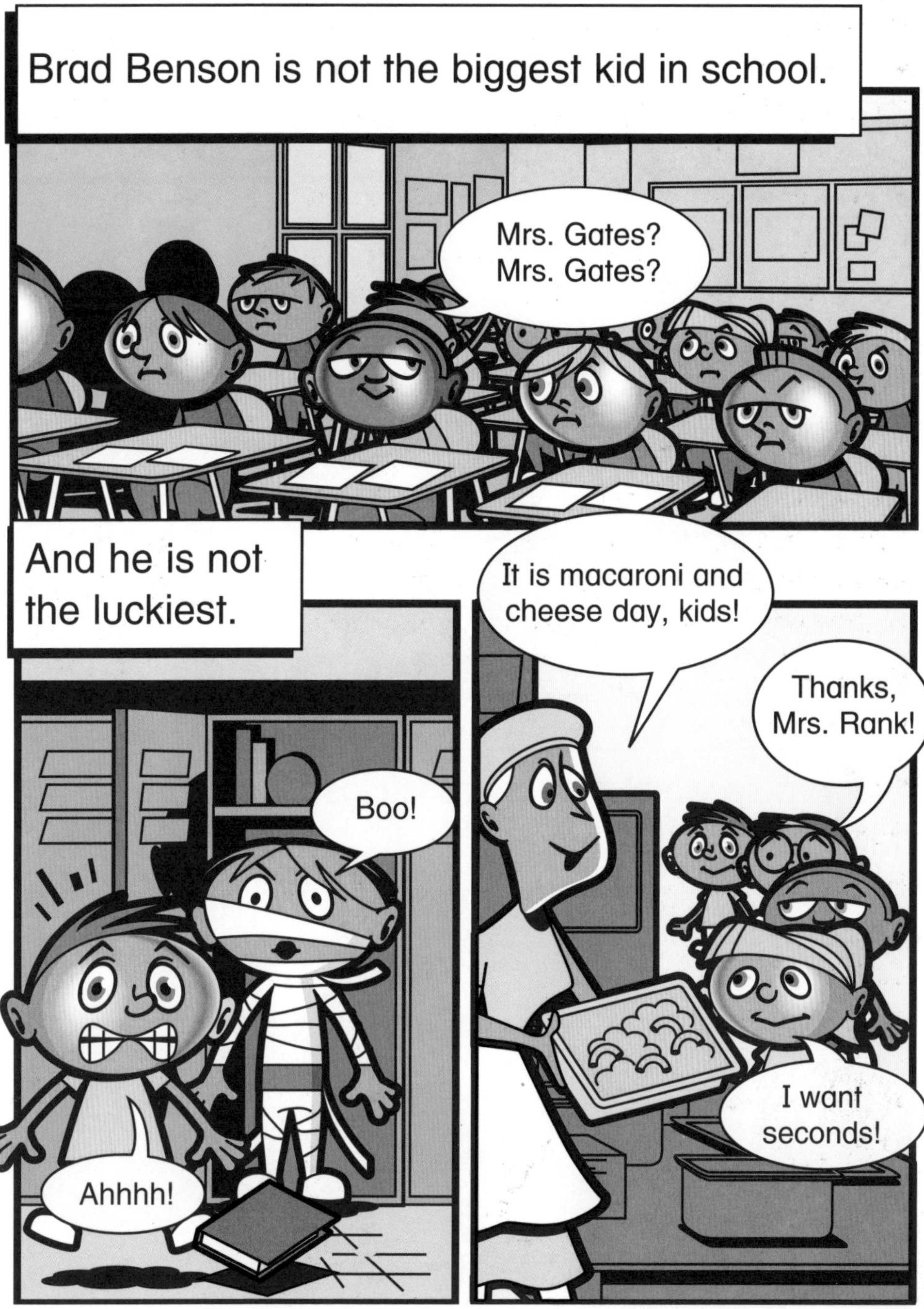
Brad Benson is not the biggest kid in school.
Mrs. Gates? Mrs. Gates?
And he is not the luckiest.
Boo!
Ahhhh!
It is macaroni and cheese day, kids!
Thanks, Mrs. Rank!
I want seconds!

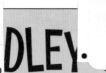

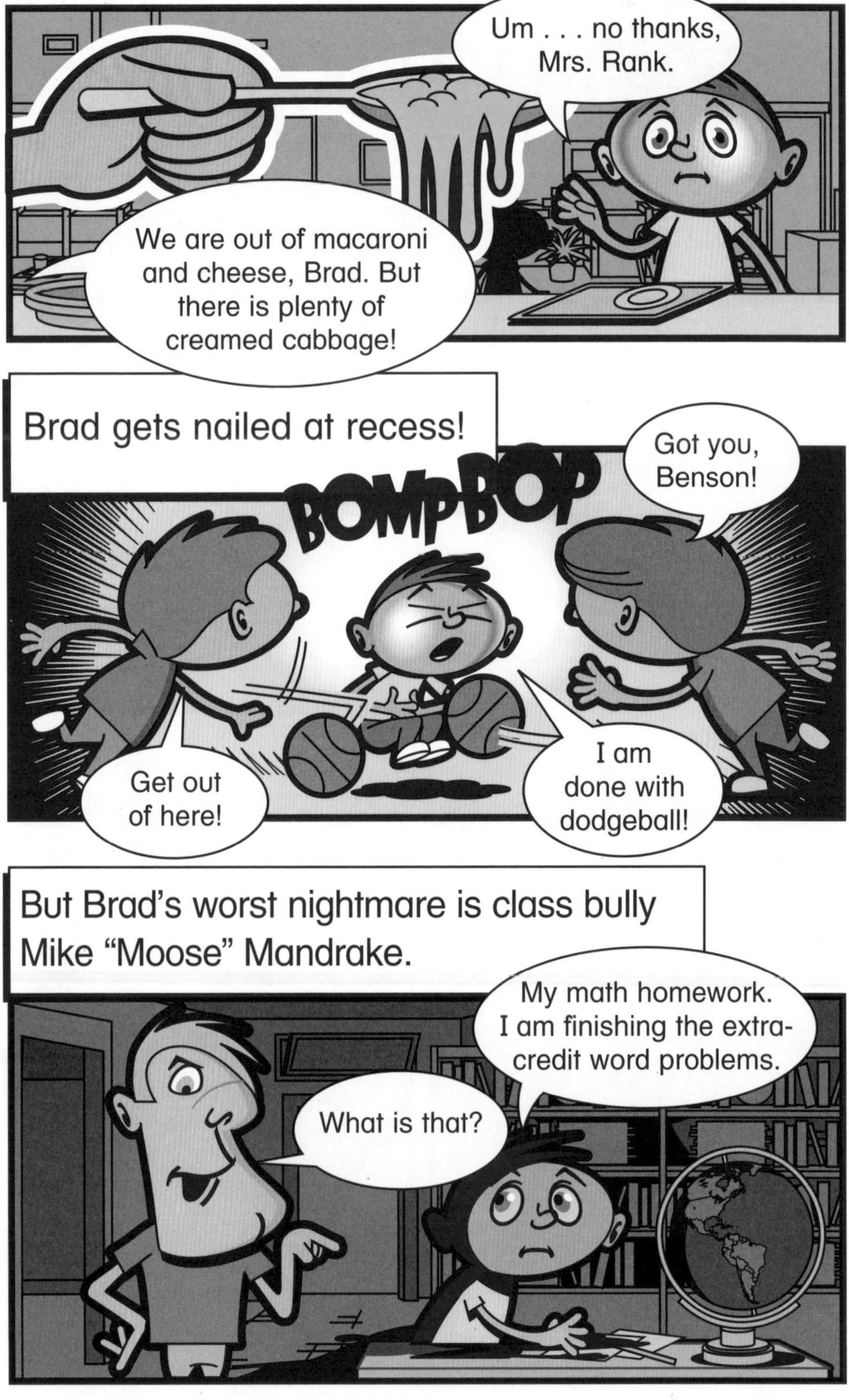
We are out of macaroni and cheese, Brad. But there is plenty of creamed cabbage!
Um . . . no thanks, Mrs. Rank.
Brad gets nailed at recess!
BOMP BOP
Got you, Benson!
Get out of here!
I am done with dodgeball!
But Brad's worst nightmare is class bully Mike "Moose" Mandrake.
What is that?
My math homework. I am finishing the extra-credit word problems.

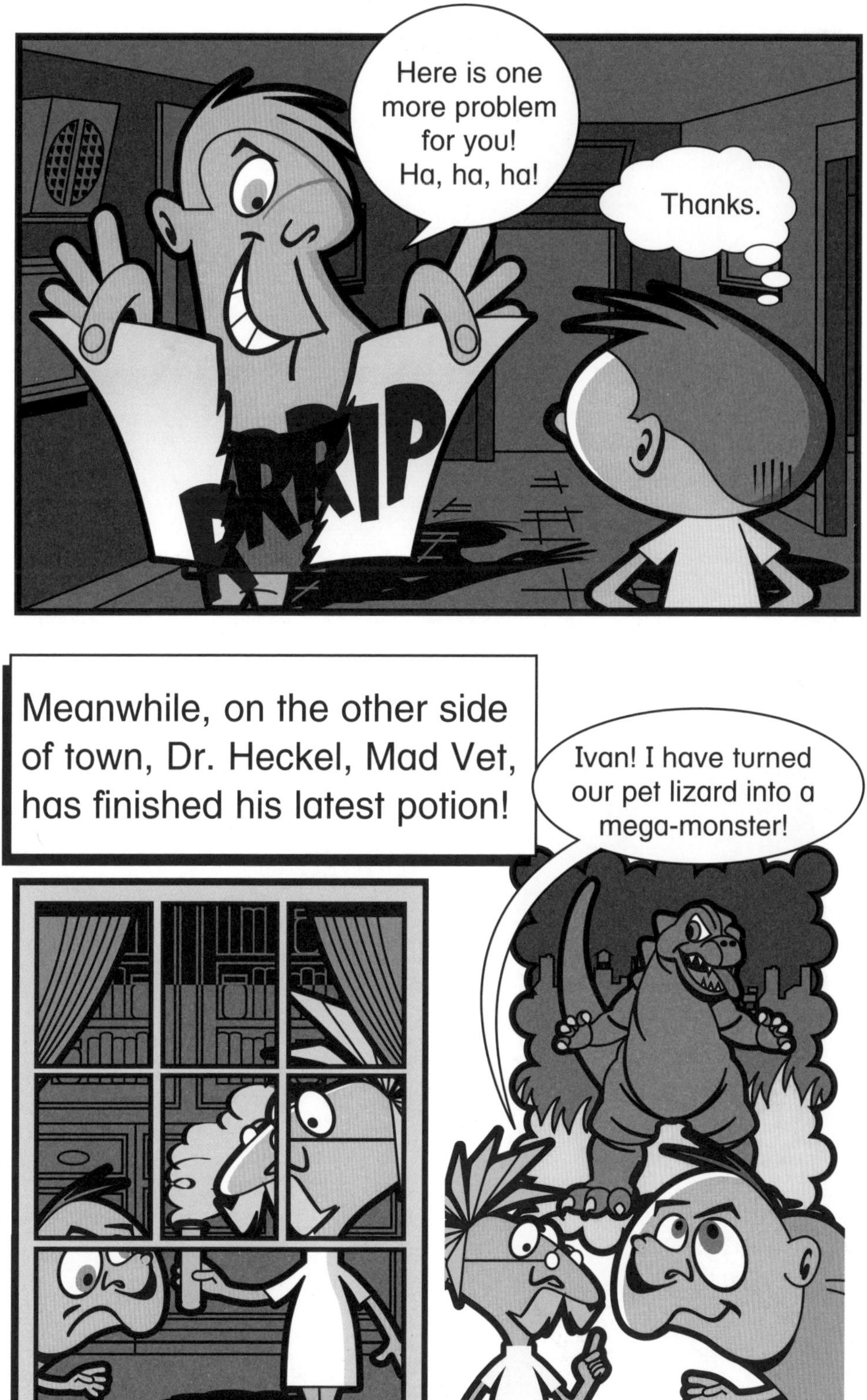
Here is one more problem for you! Ha, ha, ha!
Thanks.
RRRIP
Meanwhile, on the other side of town, Dr. Heckel, Mad Vet, has finished his latest potion!
Ivan! I have turned our pet lizard into a mega-monster!

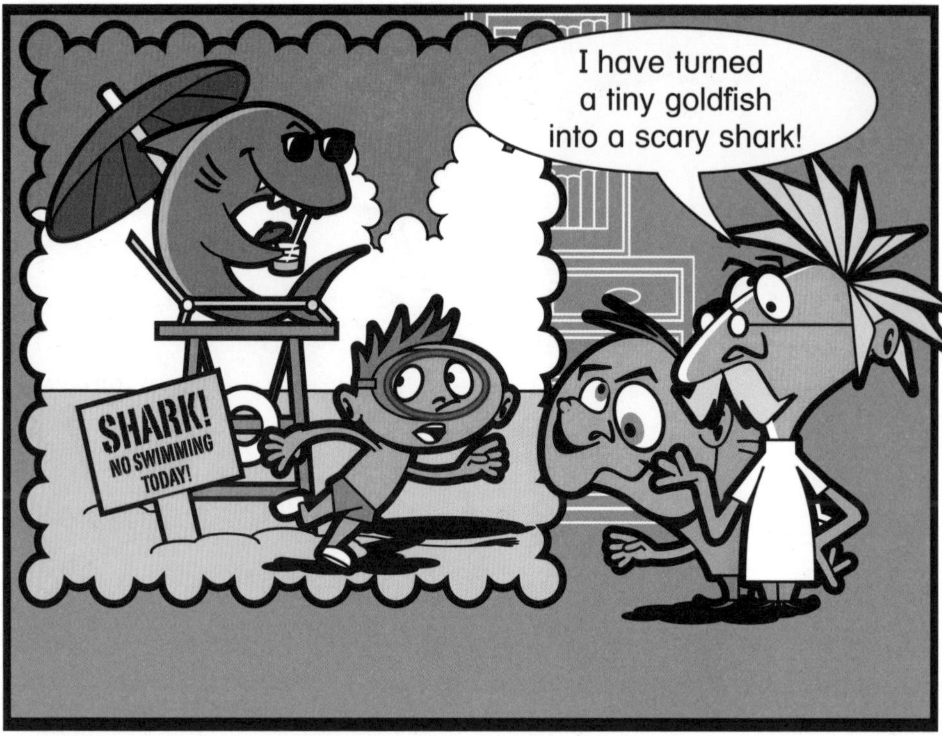
I have turned a tiny goldfish into a scary shark!
SHARK! NO SWIMMING TODAY!

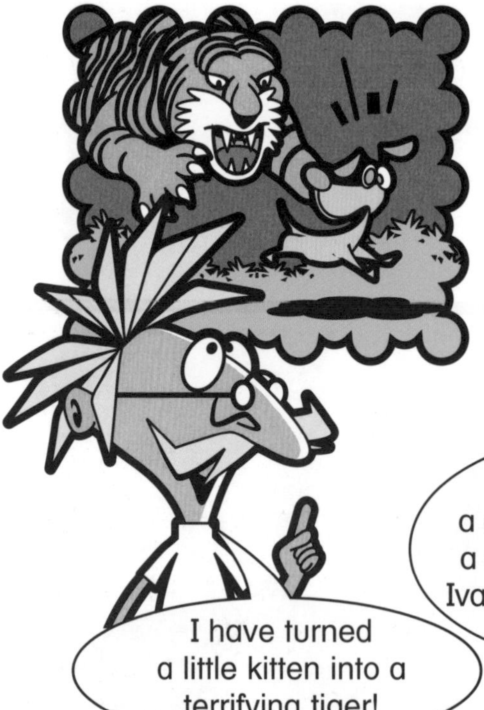
I have turned a little kitten into a terrifying tiger!

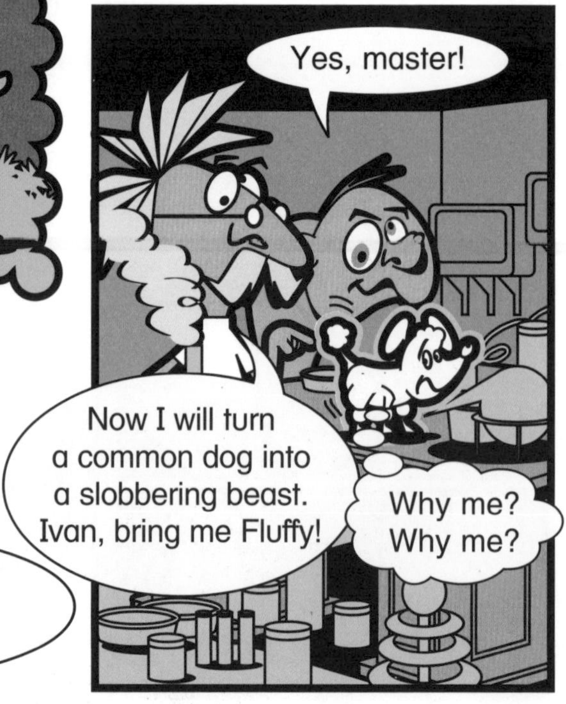
Yes, master!
Now I will turn a common dog into a slobbering beast. Ivan, bring me Fluffy!
Why me? Why me?

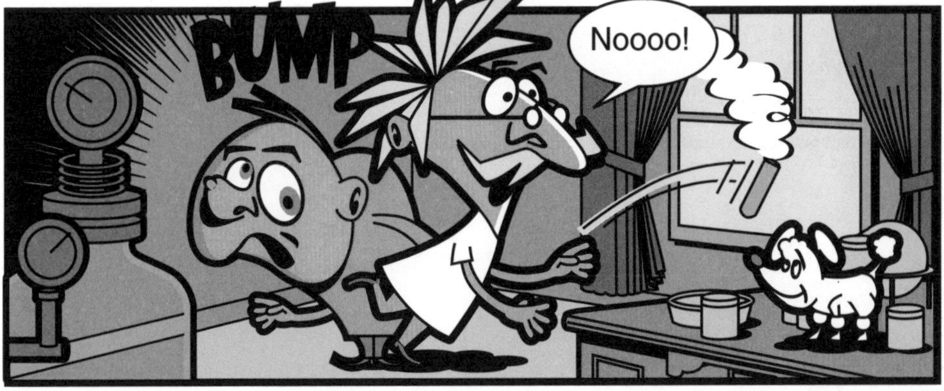
BUMP
Noooo!

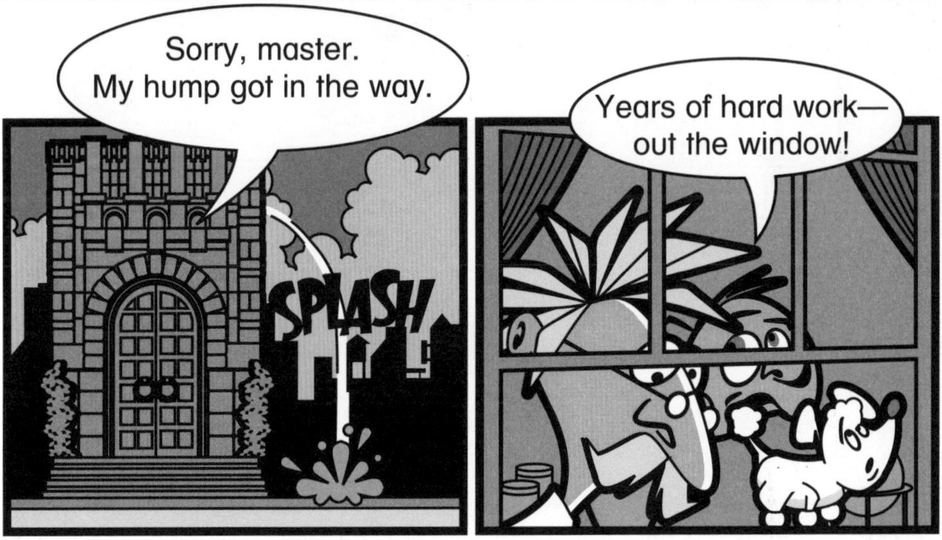
Sorry, master.
My hump got in the way.
SPLASH
Years of hard work—
out the window!

Dr. Heckel is not the only one having a bad day . . . Brad misses the bus!

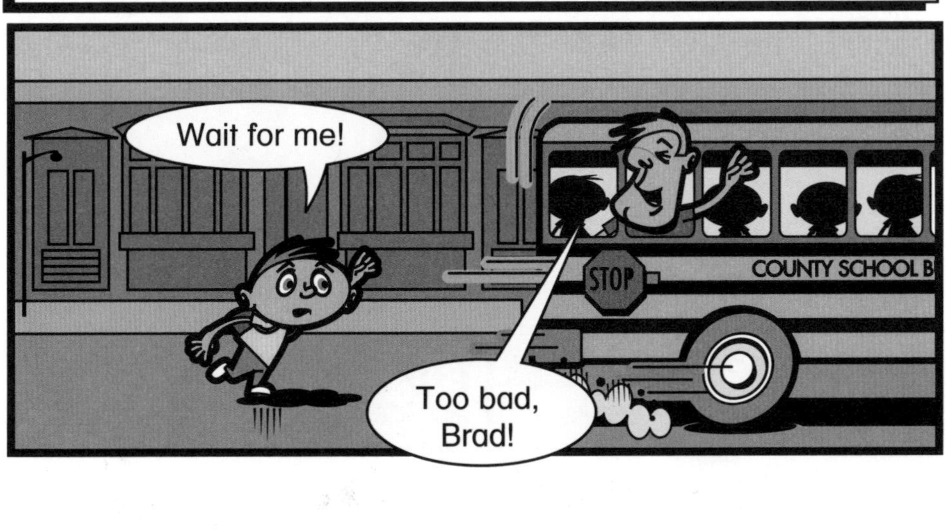
Wait for me!
STOP
COUNTY SCHOOL
Too bad,
Brad!

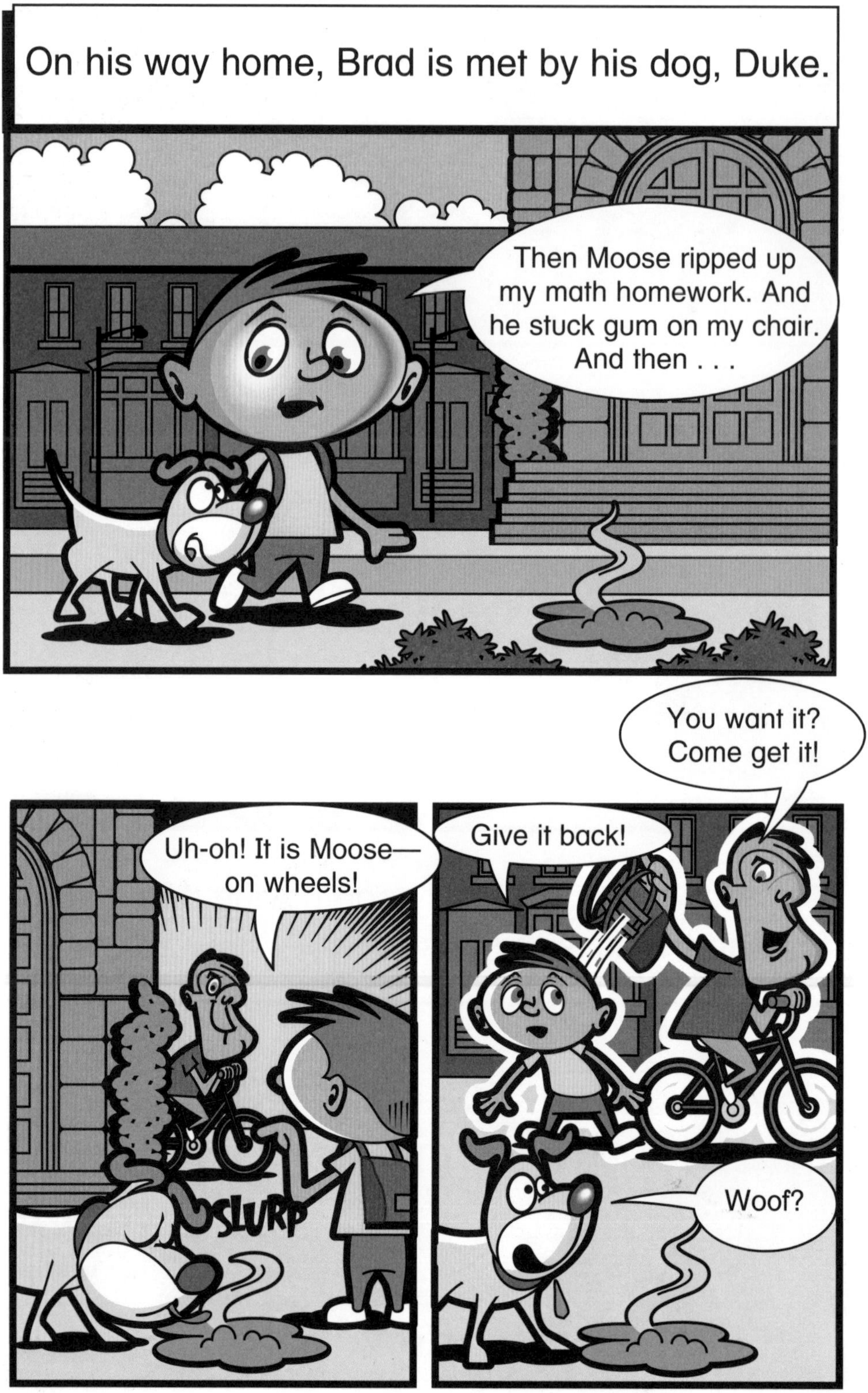
On his way home, Brad is met by his dog, Duke.
Then Moose ripped up my math homework. And he stuck gum on my chair. And then . . .
Uh-oh! It is Moose— on wheels!
SLURP
Give it back!
You want it? Come get it!
Woof?

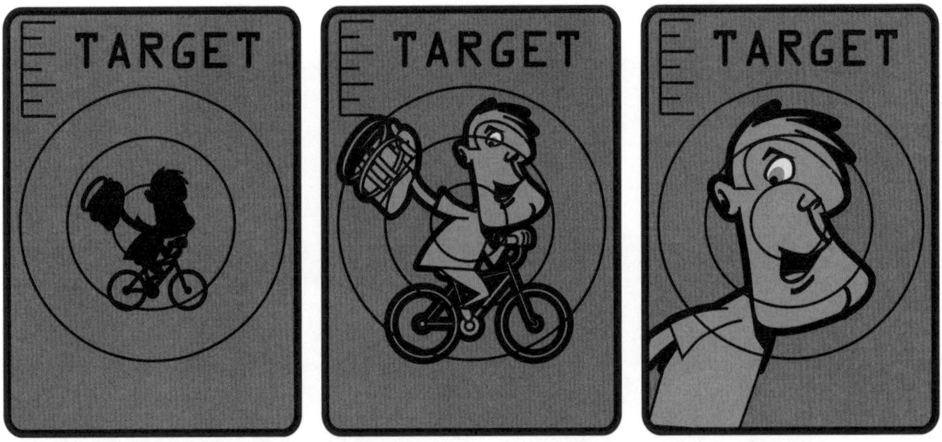
TARGET
TARGET
TARGET

Duke starts to change . . . he grows fangs!

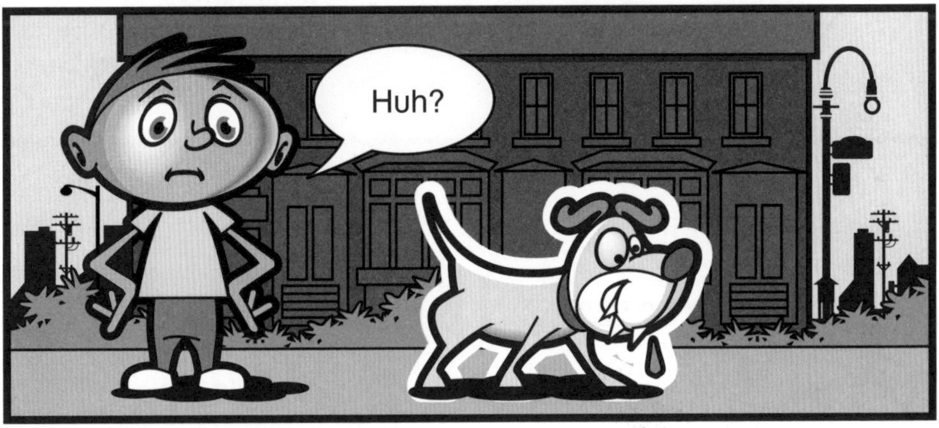
Huh?

Duke grows strong!

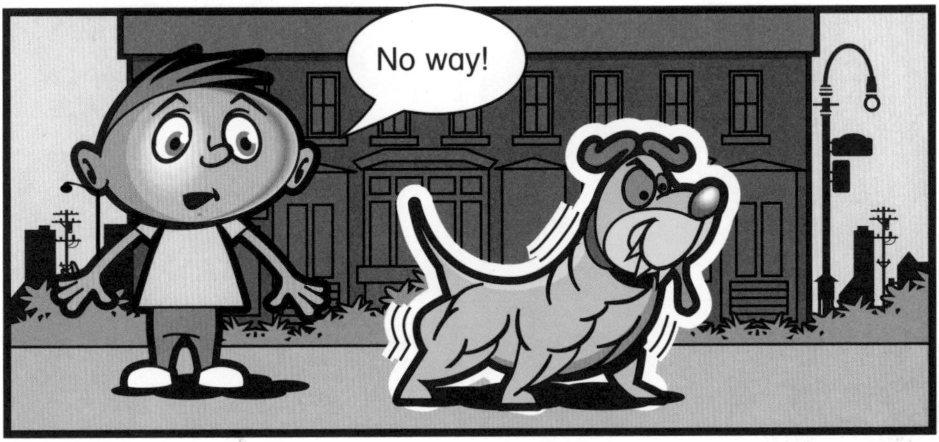
No way!

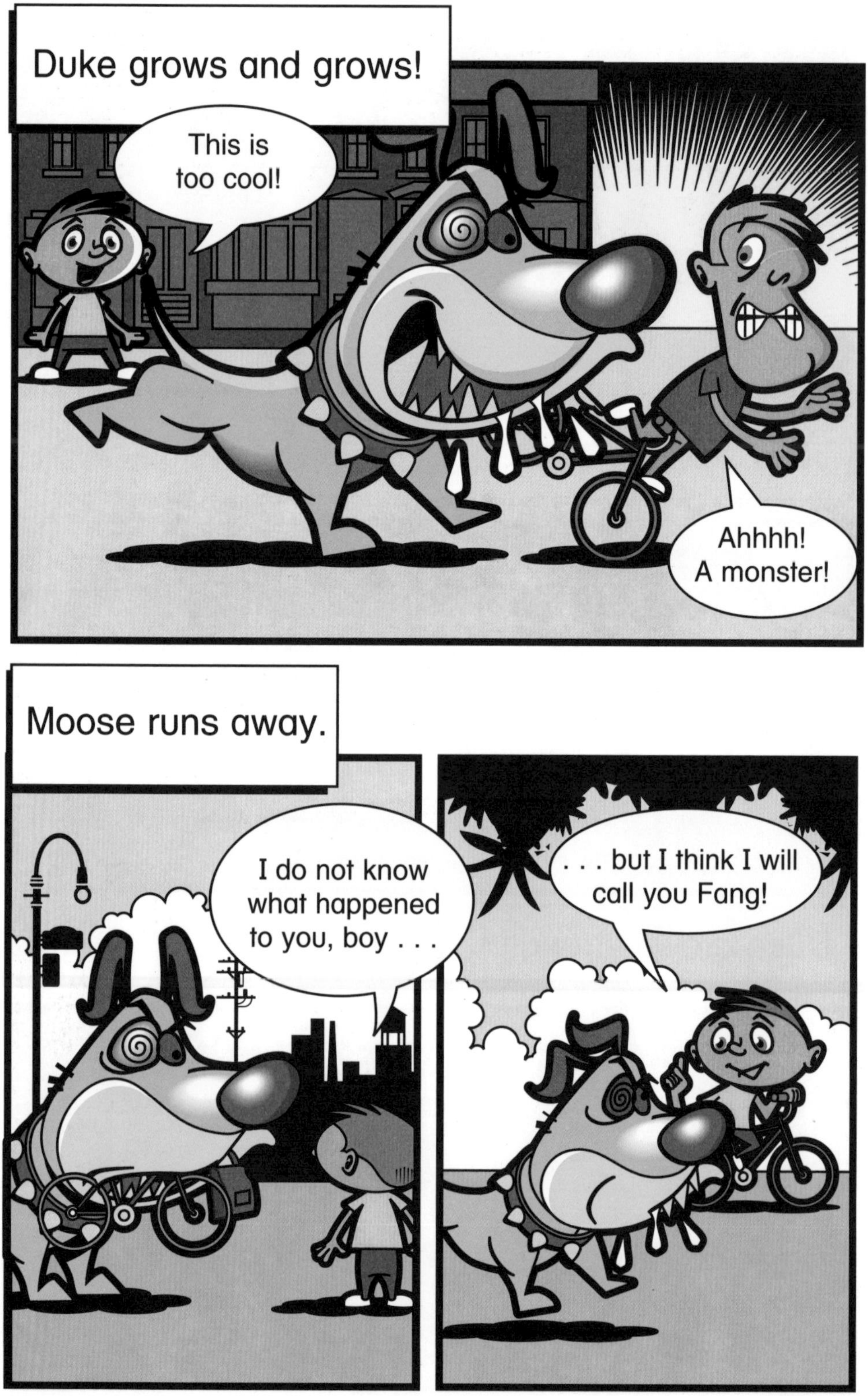
Duke grows and grows!
This is too cool!
Ahhhh! A monster!
Moose runs away.
I do not know what happened to you, boy . . .
. . . but I think I will call you Fang!

FANGS FOR NOTHING!

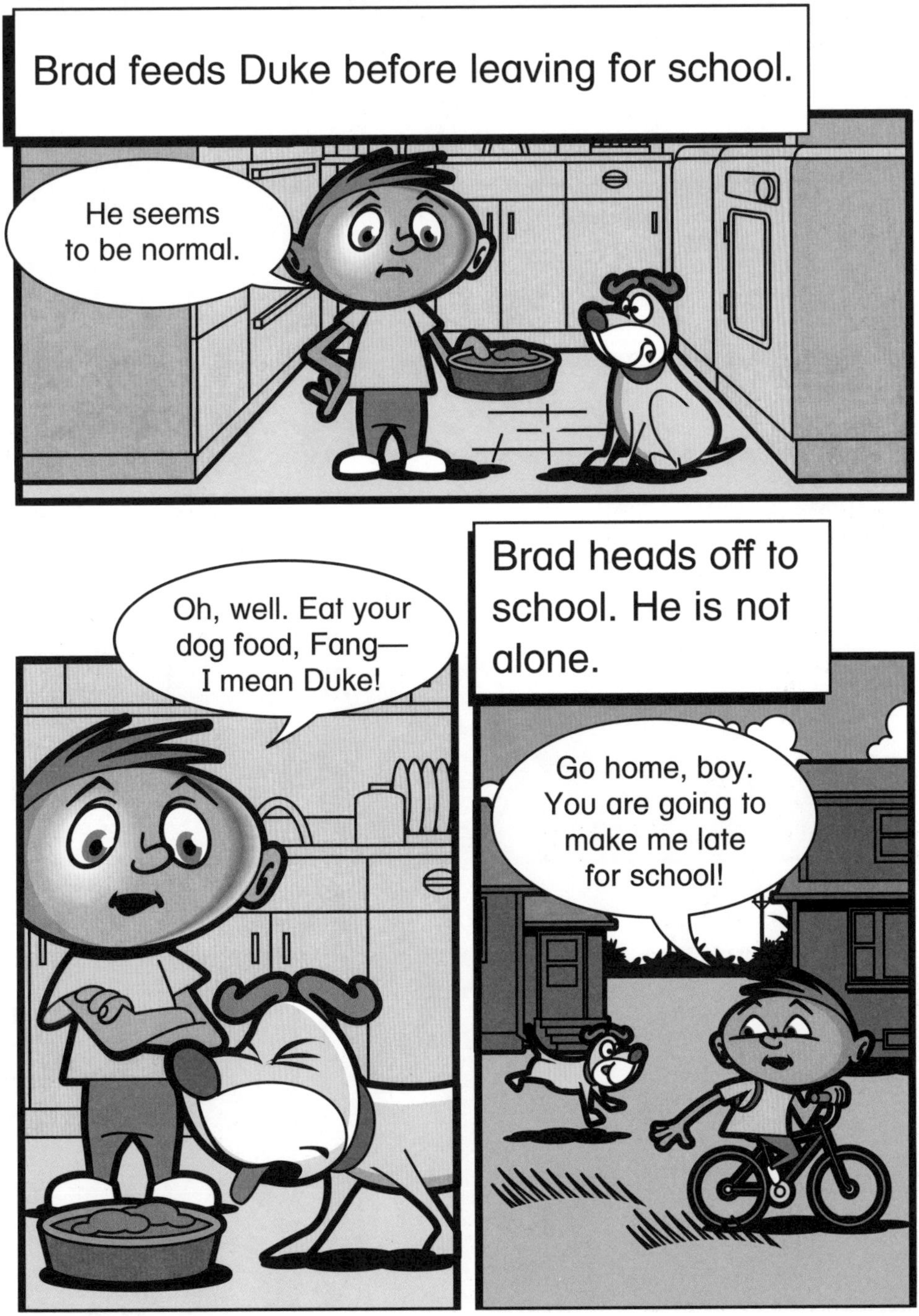
Brad feeds Duke before leaving for school.
He seems to be normal.
Oh, well. Eat your dog food, Fang— I mean Duke!
Brad heads off to school. He is not alone.
Go home, boy. You are going to make me late for school!

At school, Brad's teacher is on his case.

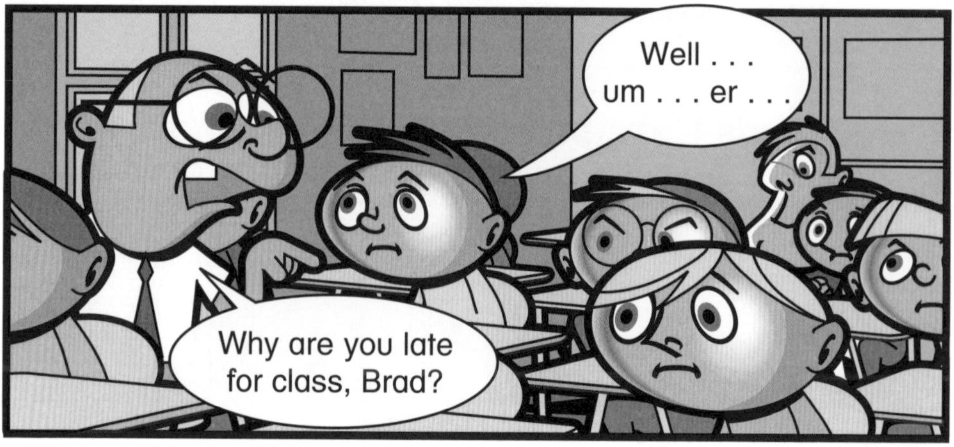
Why are you late
for class, Brad?
Well . . .
um . . . er . . .

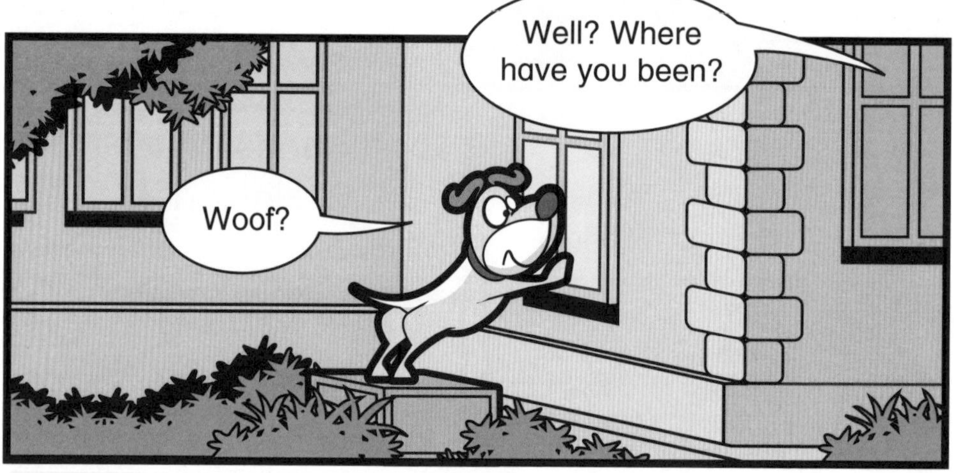
Well? Where
have you been?
Woof?

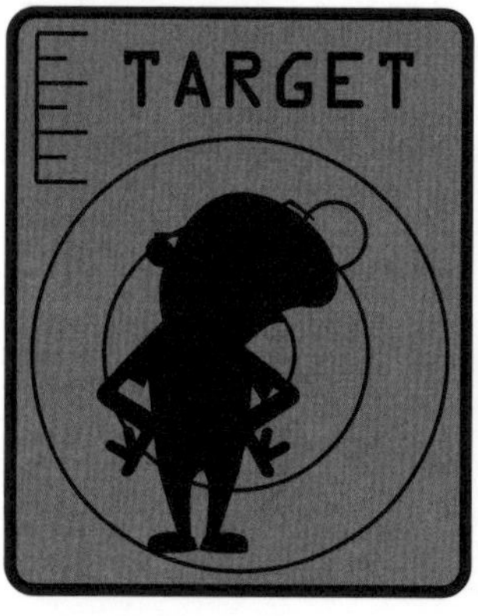
TARGET

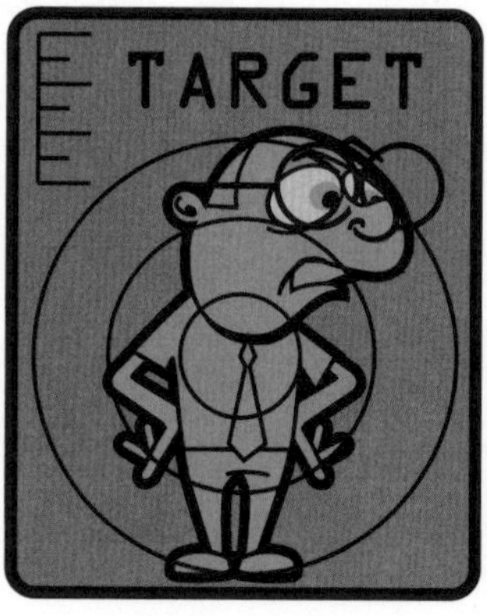
TARGET

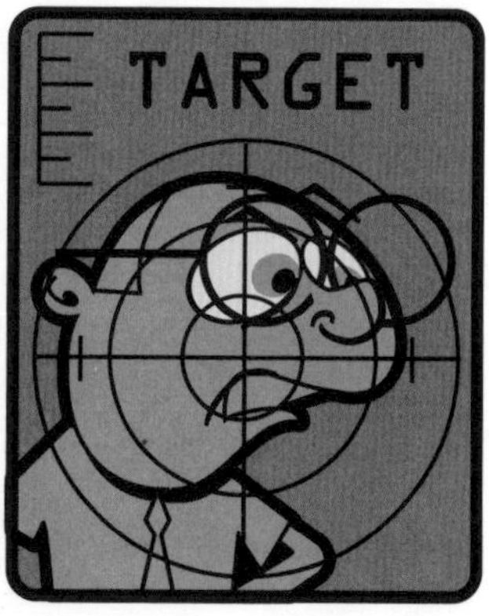
TARGET

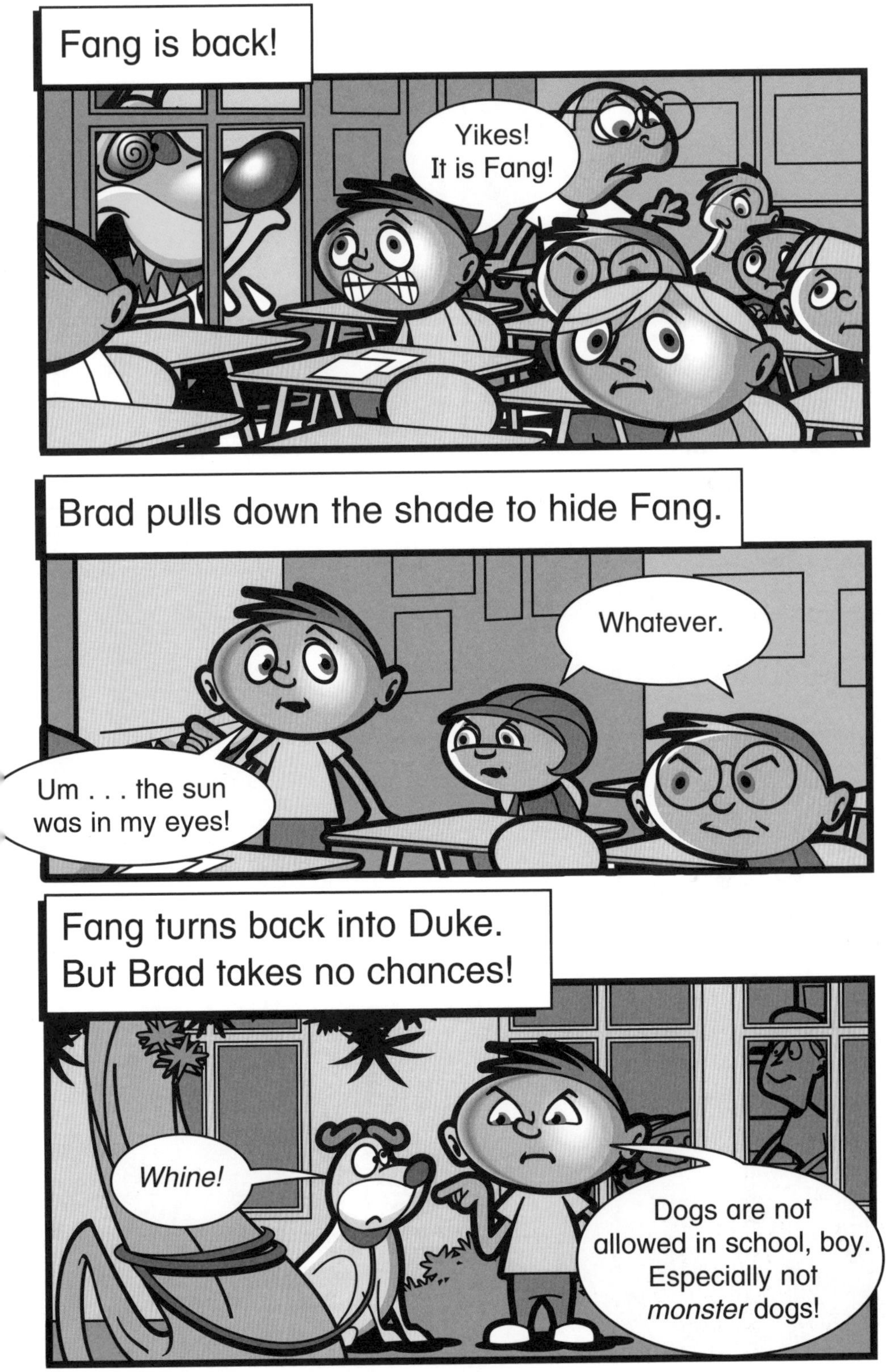
Fang is back!
Yikes!
It is Fang!
Brad pulls down the shade to hide Fang.
Um . . . the sun
was in my eyes!
Whatever.
Fang turns back into Duke.
But Brad takes no chances!
Whine!
Dogs are not
allowed in school, boy.
Especially not
monster dogs!

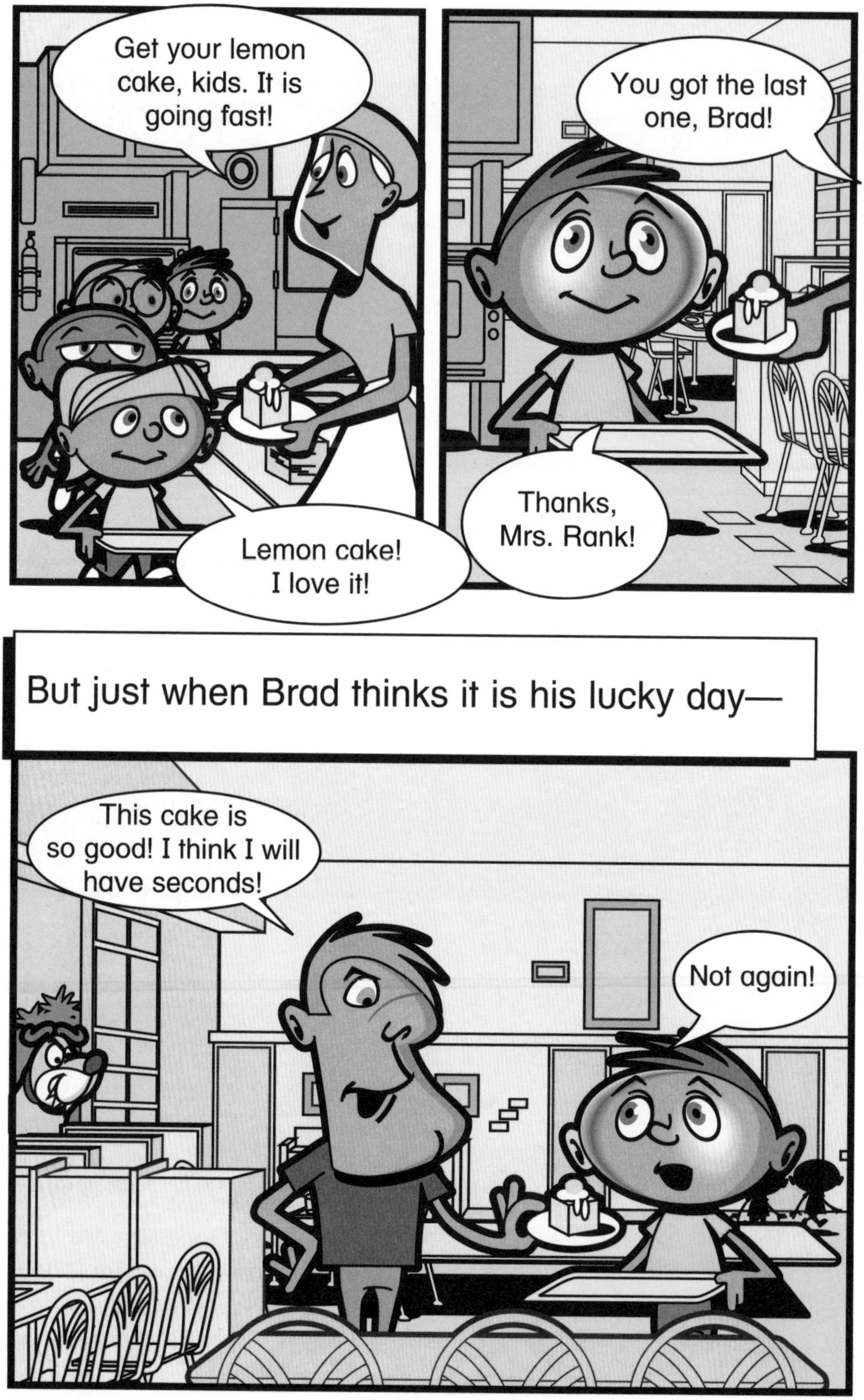
Get your lemon cake, kids. It is going fast!
Lemon cake! I love it!
You got the last one, Brad!
Thanks, Mrs. Rank!
But just when Brad thinks it is his lucky day—
This cake is so good! I think I will have seconds!
Not again!

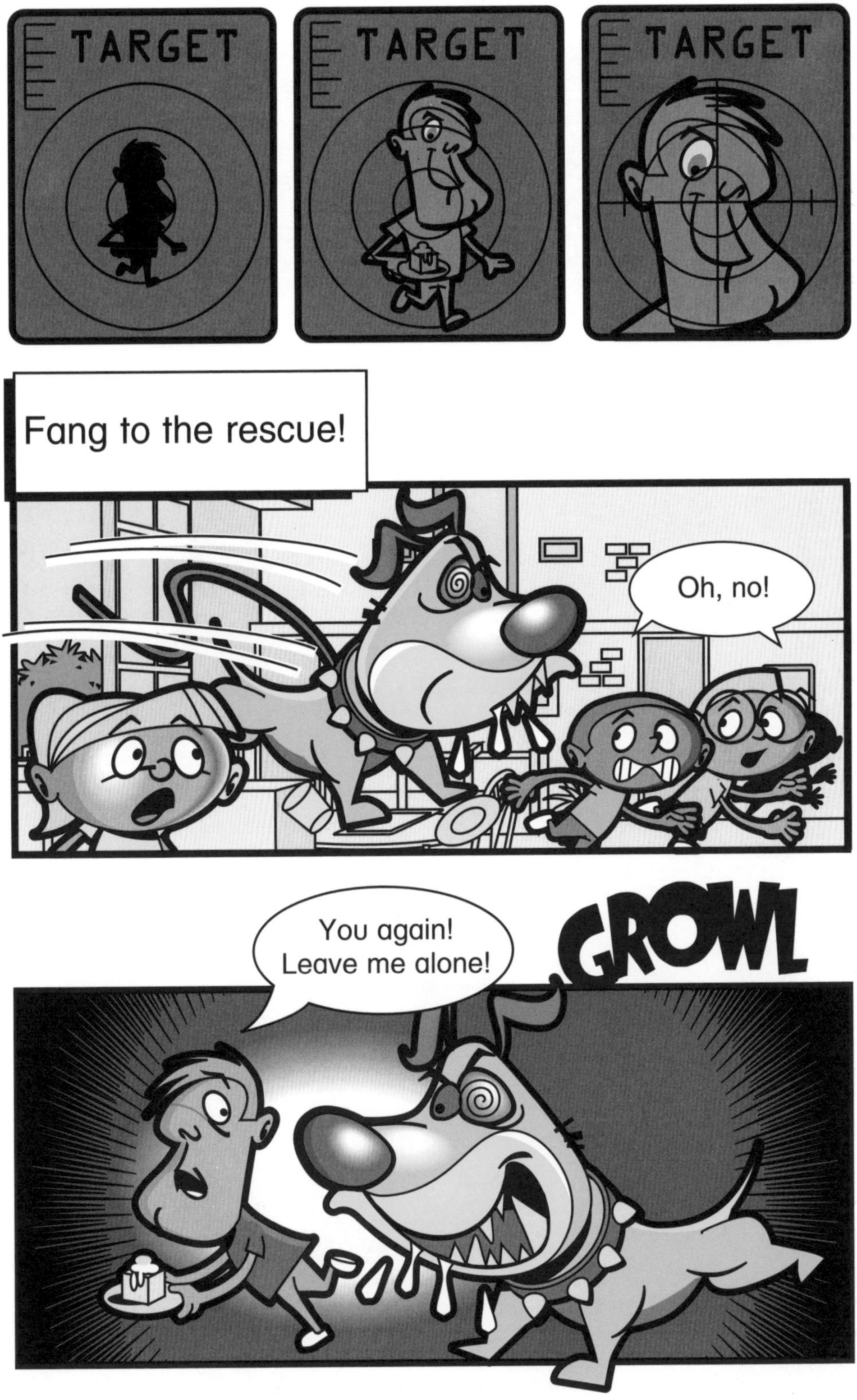
TARGET
TARGET
TARGET
Fang to the rescue!
Oh, no!
You again!
Leave me alone!
GROWL

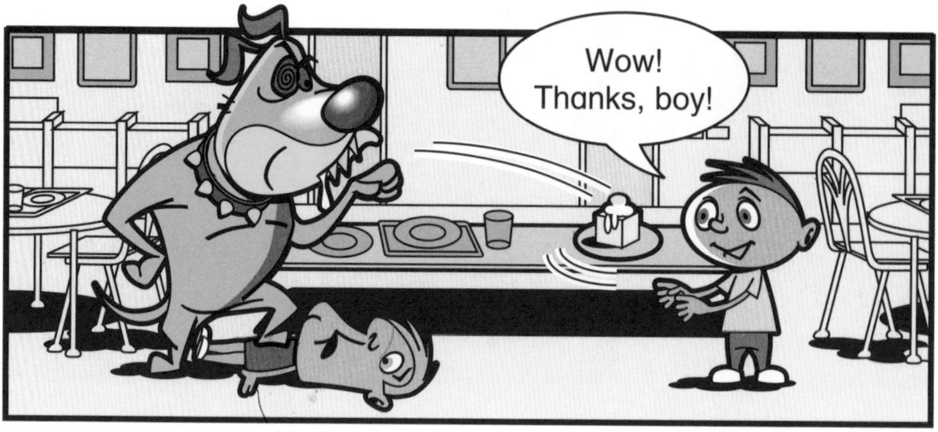
Wow!
Thanks, boy!

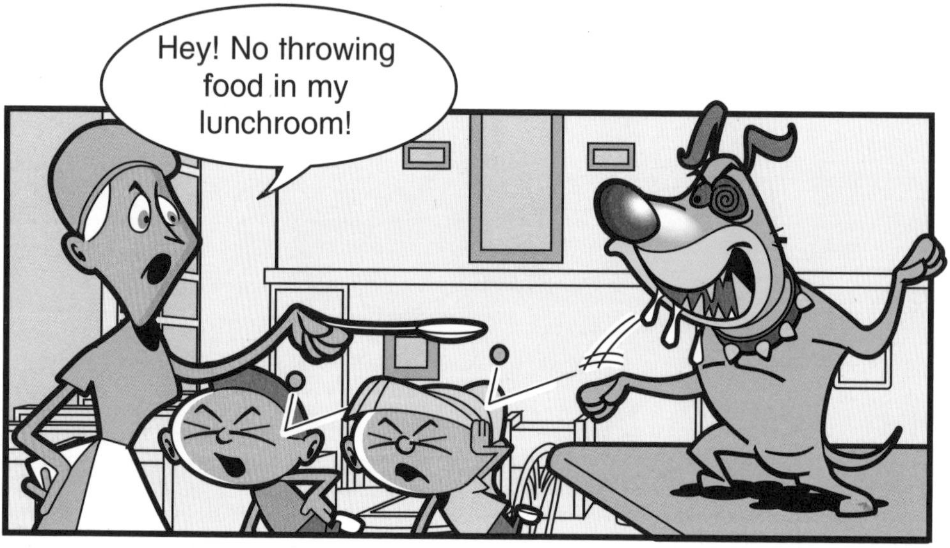
Hey! No throwing
food in my
lunchroom!

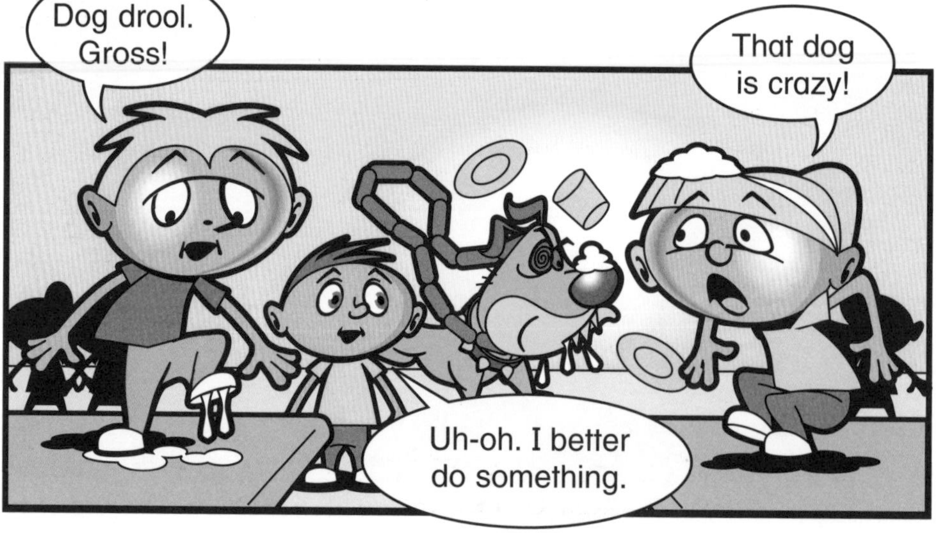
Dog drool.
Gross!
That dog
is crazy!
Uh-oh. I better
do something.

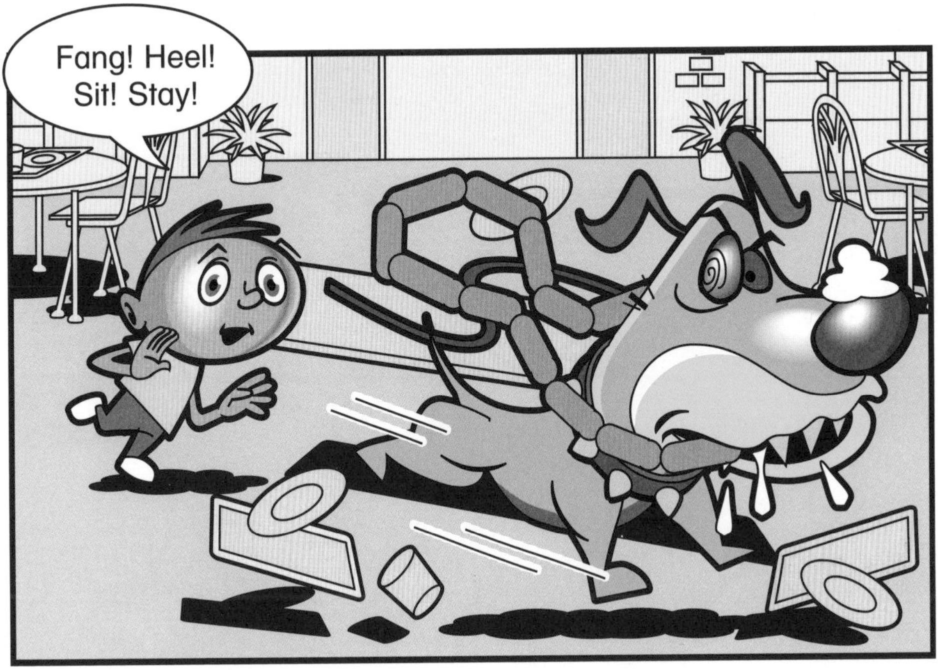
Fang! Heel! Sit! Stay!

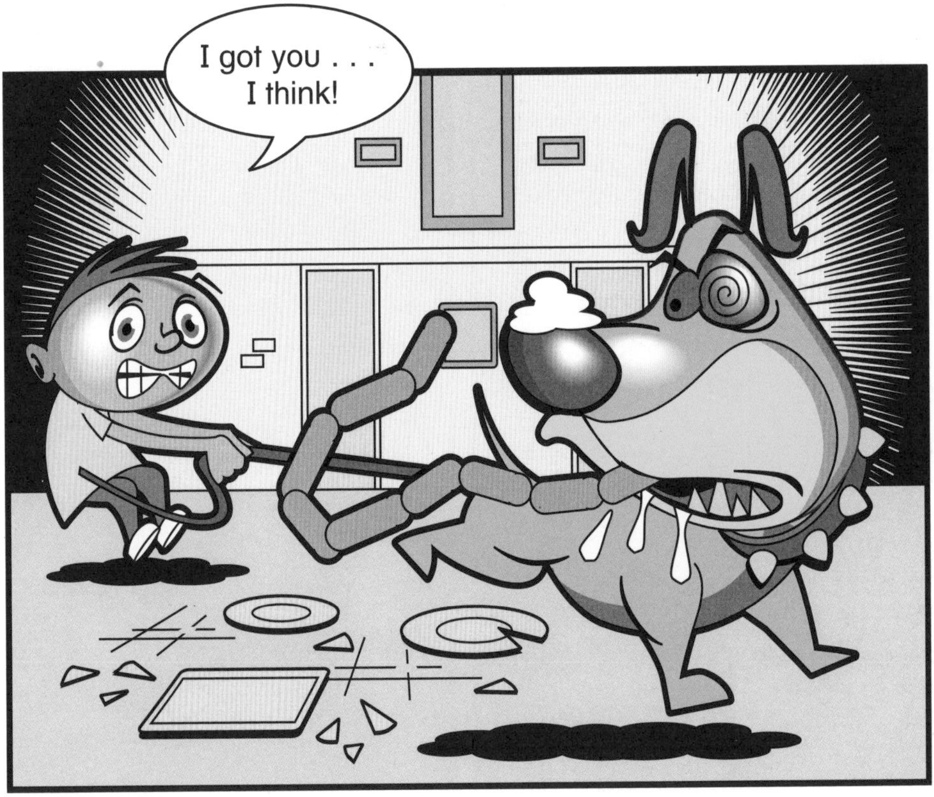
I got you . . . I think!

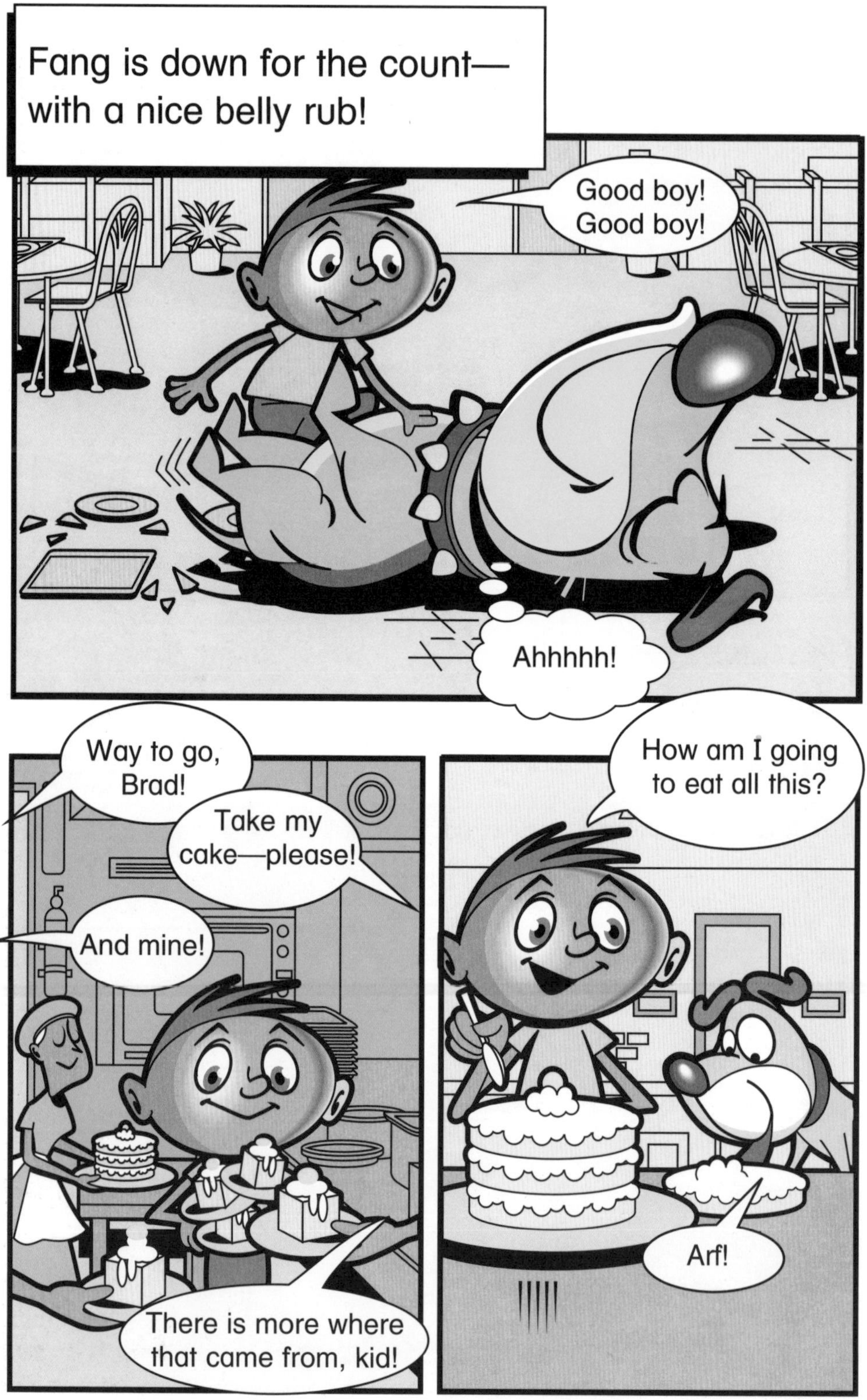
Fang is down for the count—with a nice belly rub!
Good boy! Good boy!
Ahhhhh!
Way to go, Brad!
Take my cake—please!
And mine!
There is more where that came from, kid!
How am I going to eat all this?
Arf!

MAD SCIENCE

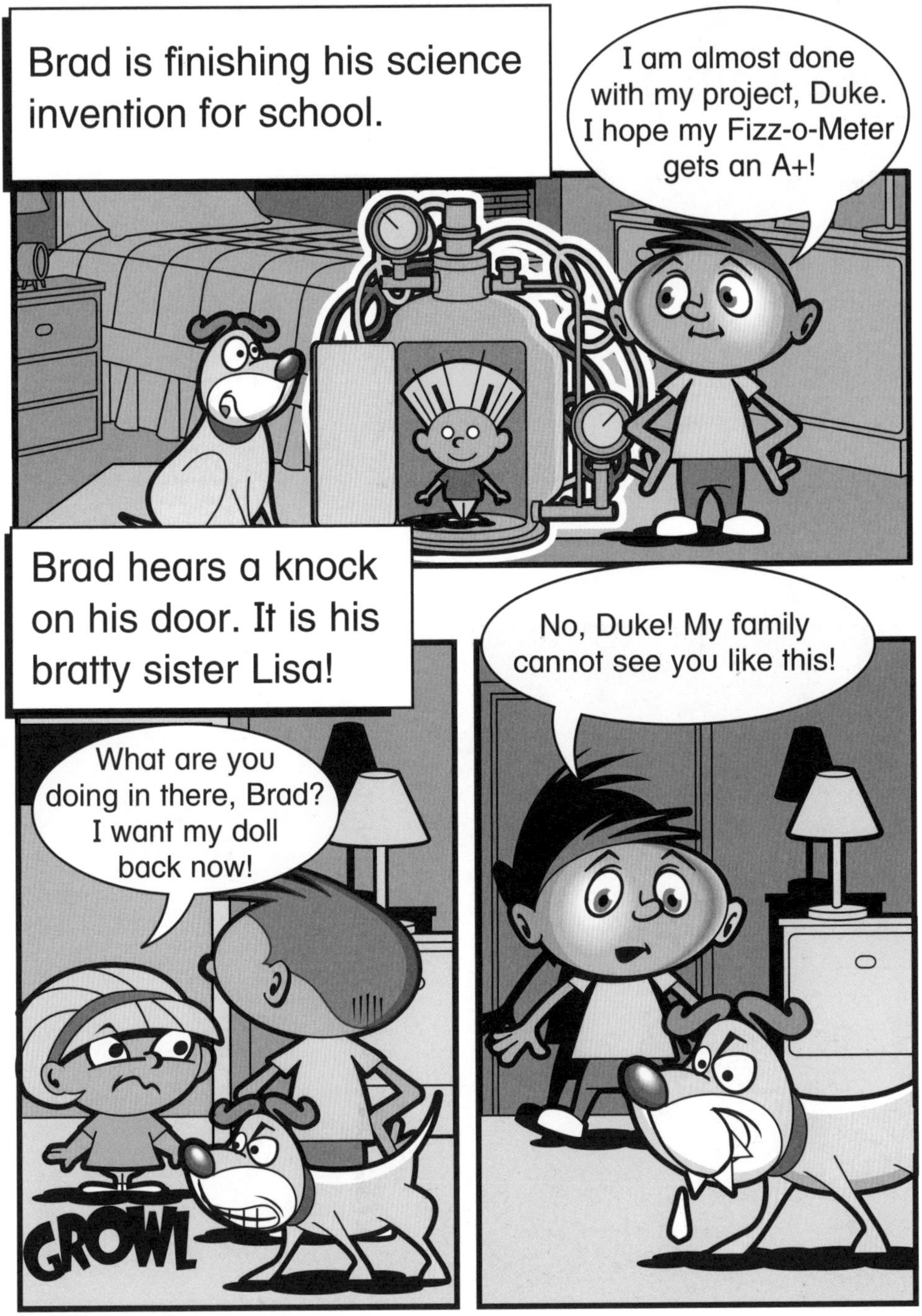
Brad is finishing his science invention for school.
I am almost done with my project, Duke. I hope my Fizz-o-Meter gets an A+!
Brad hears a knock on his door. It is his bratty sister Lisa!
What are you doing in there, Brad? I want my doll back now!
GROWL
No, Duke! My family cannot see you like this!

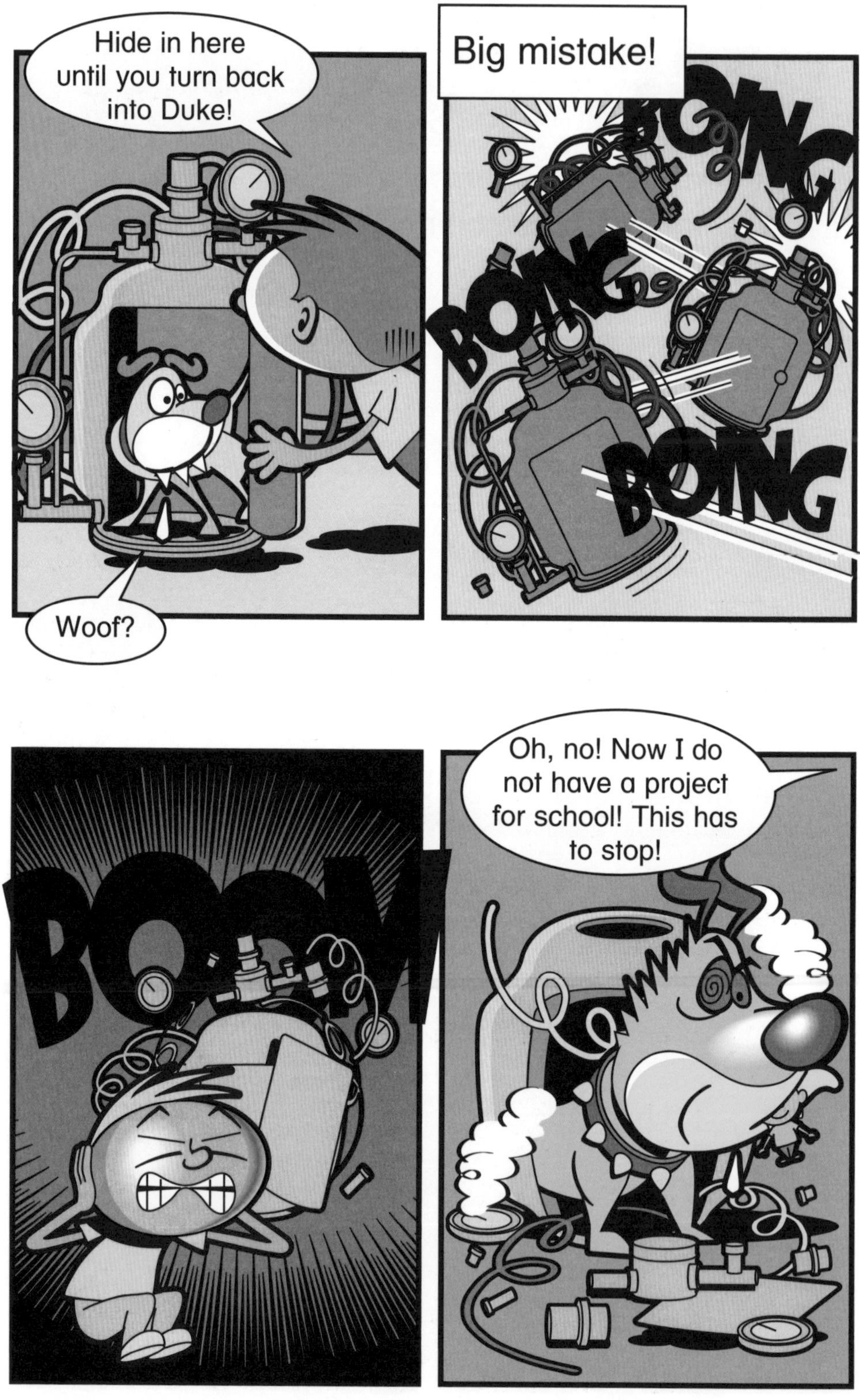
Hide in here
until you turn back
into Duke!
Woof?
Big mistake!
BOING
BOING
BOING
BOOM!
Oh, no! Now I do
not have a project
for school! This has
to stop!

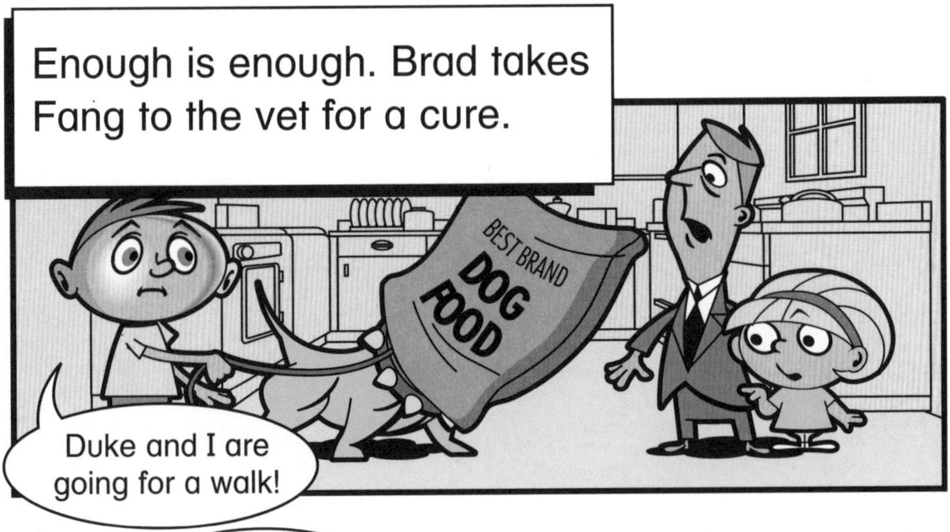
Enough is enough. Brad takes Fang to the vet for a cure.
BEST BRAND DOG FOOD
Duke and I are going for a walk!

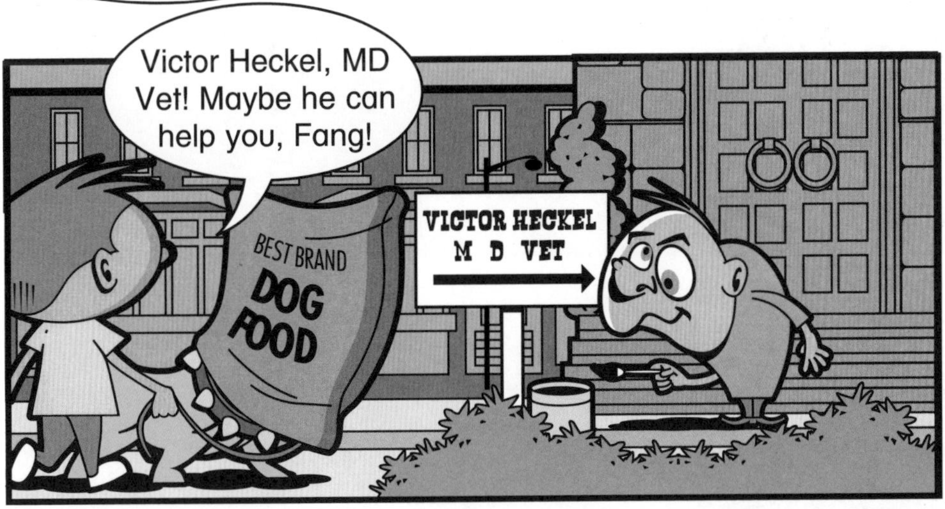
Victor Heckel, MD Vet! Maybe he can help you, Fang!
BEST BRAND DOG FOOD
VICTOR HECKEL
M D VET

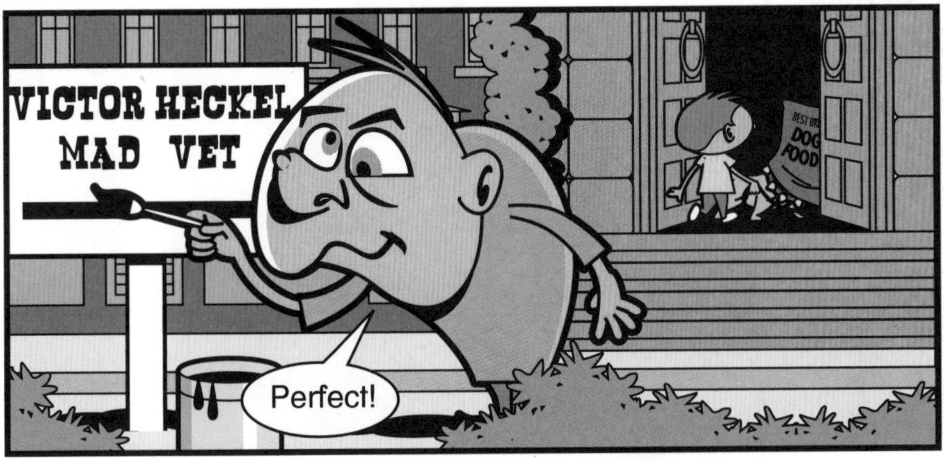
VICTOR HECKEL
MAD VET
Perfect!

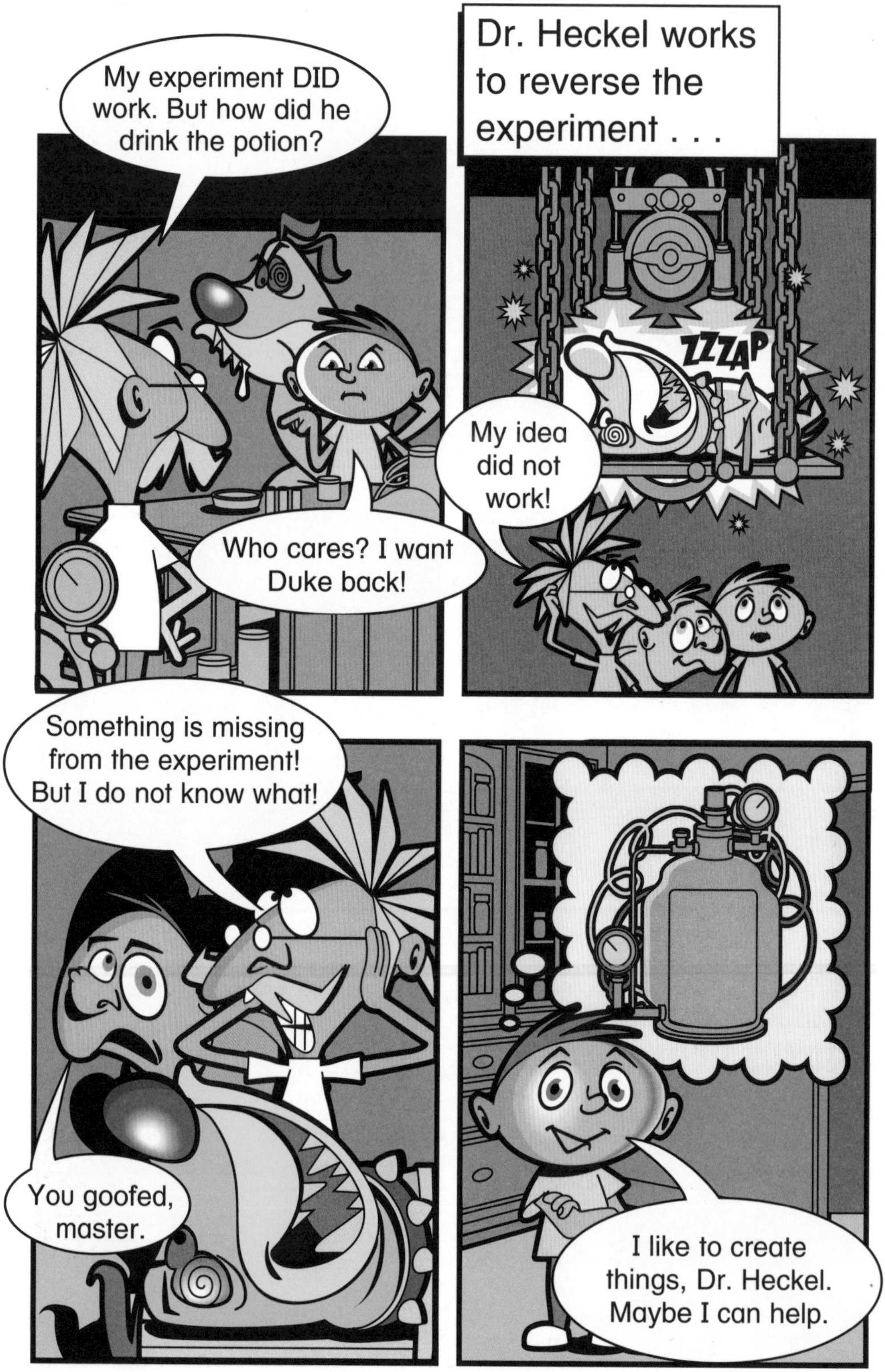
My experiment DID work. But how did he drink the potion?
Who cares? I want Duke back!
Dr. Heckel works to reverse the experiment . . .
ZZZAP
My idea did not work!
Something is missing from the experiment! But I do not know what!
You goofed, master.
I like to create things, Dr. Heckel. Maybe I can help.

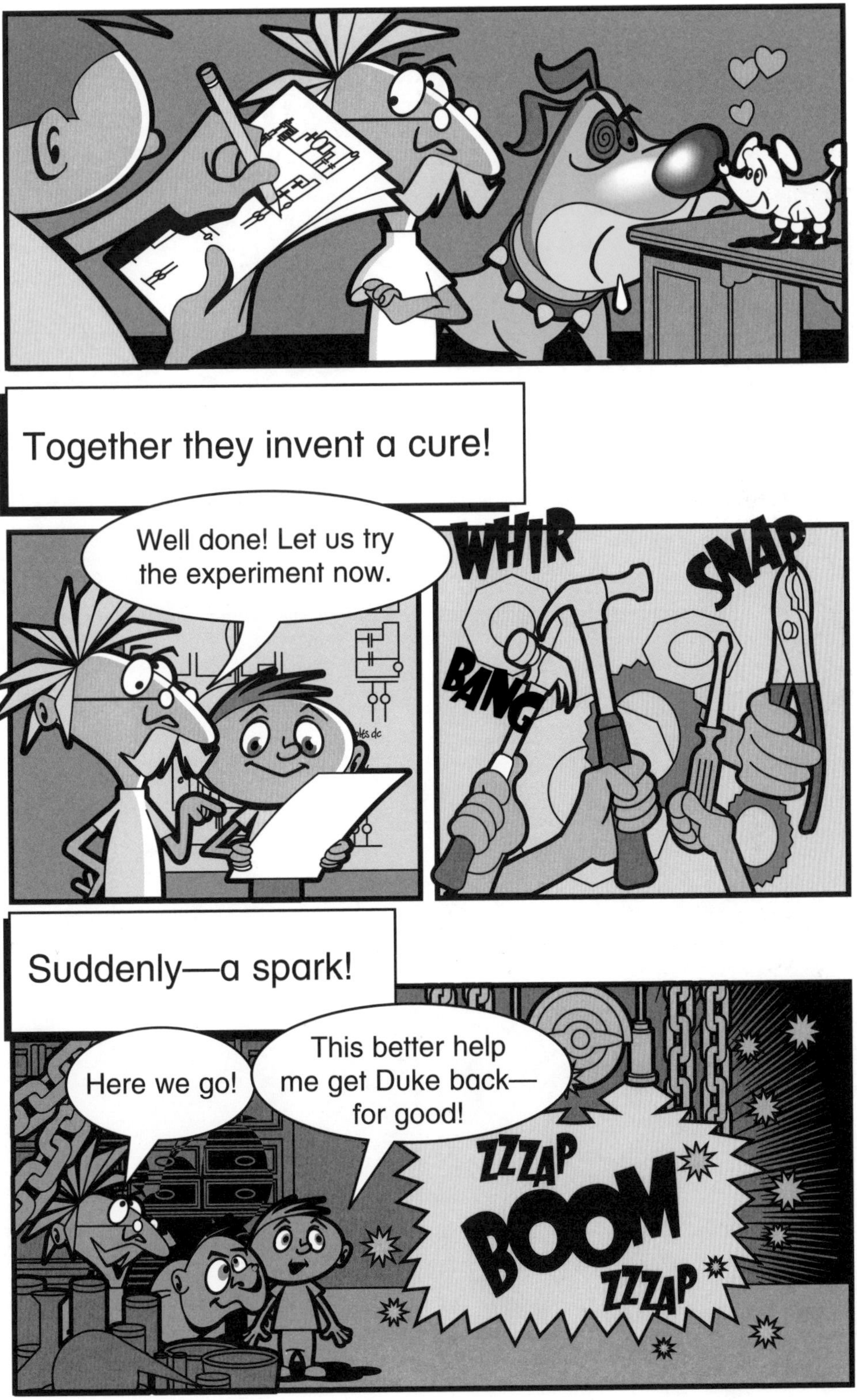
Together they invent a cure!
Well done! Let us try the experiment now.
WHIR
SNAP
BANG
Suddenly—a spark!
Here we go!
This better help me get Duke back—for good!
ZZZAP
BOOM
ZZZAP

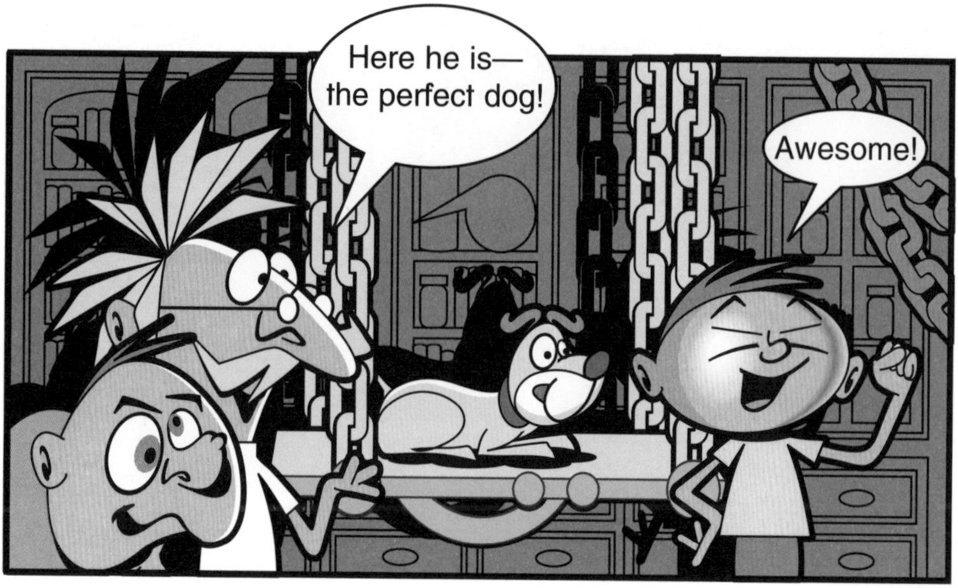
Here he is—
the perfect dog!
Awesome!

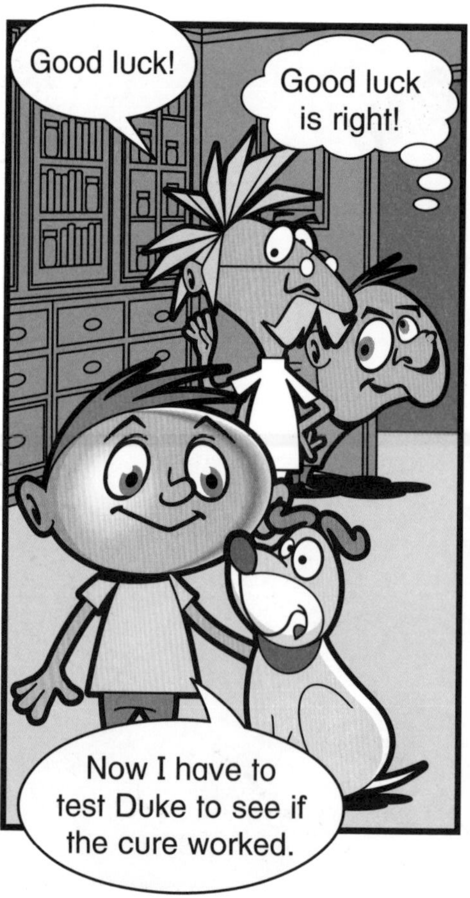
Good luck!
Good luck is right!
Now I have to test Duke to see if the cure worked.

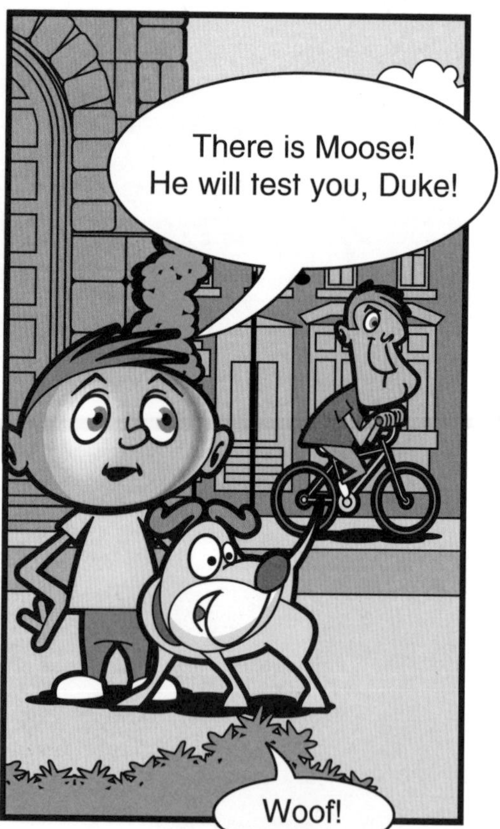
There is Moose! He will test you, Duke!
Woof!

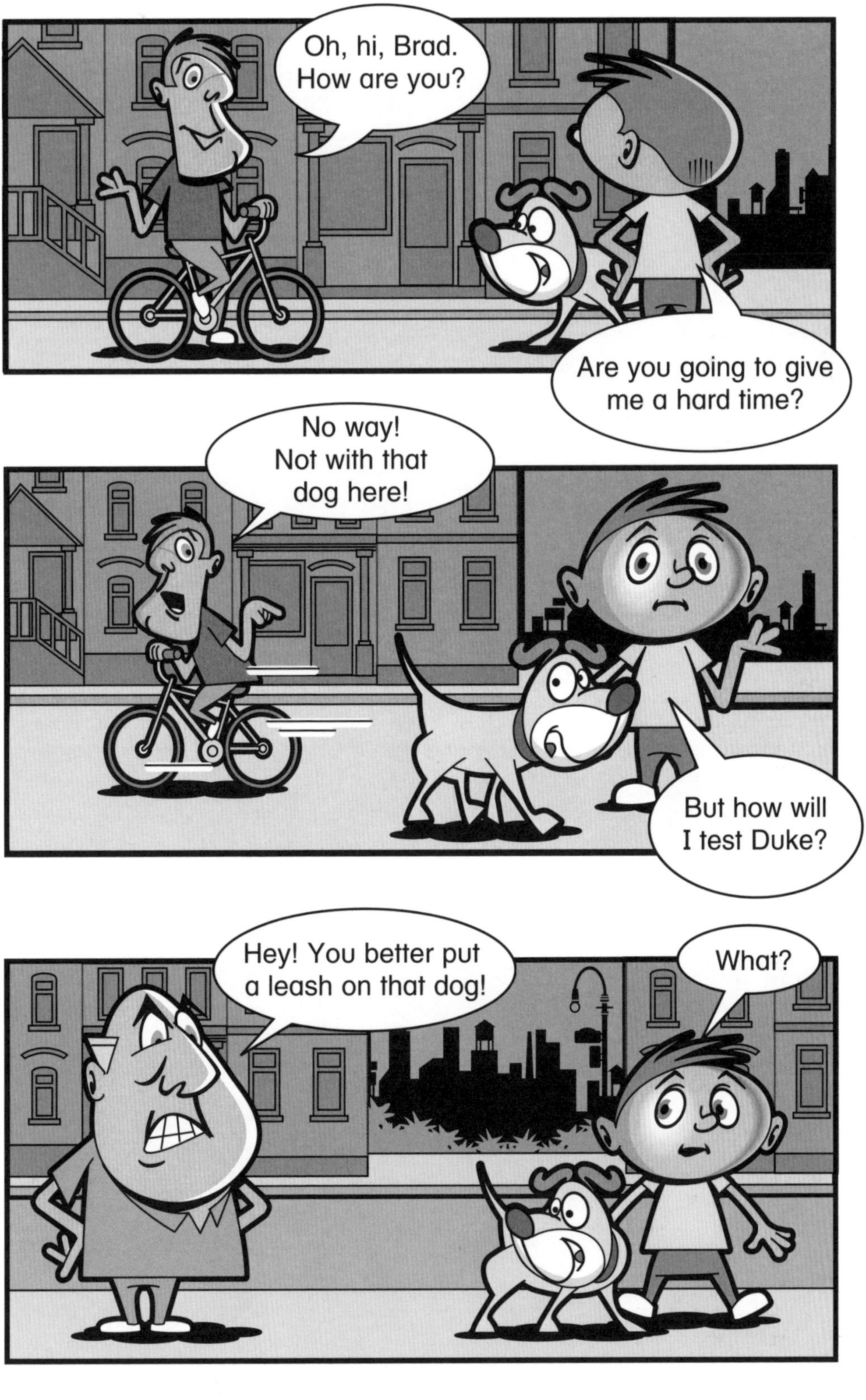
Oh, hi, Brad.
How are you?
Are you going to give
me a hard time?
No way!
Not with that
dog here!
But how will
I test Duke?
Hey! You better put
a leash on that dog!
What?

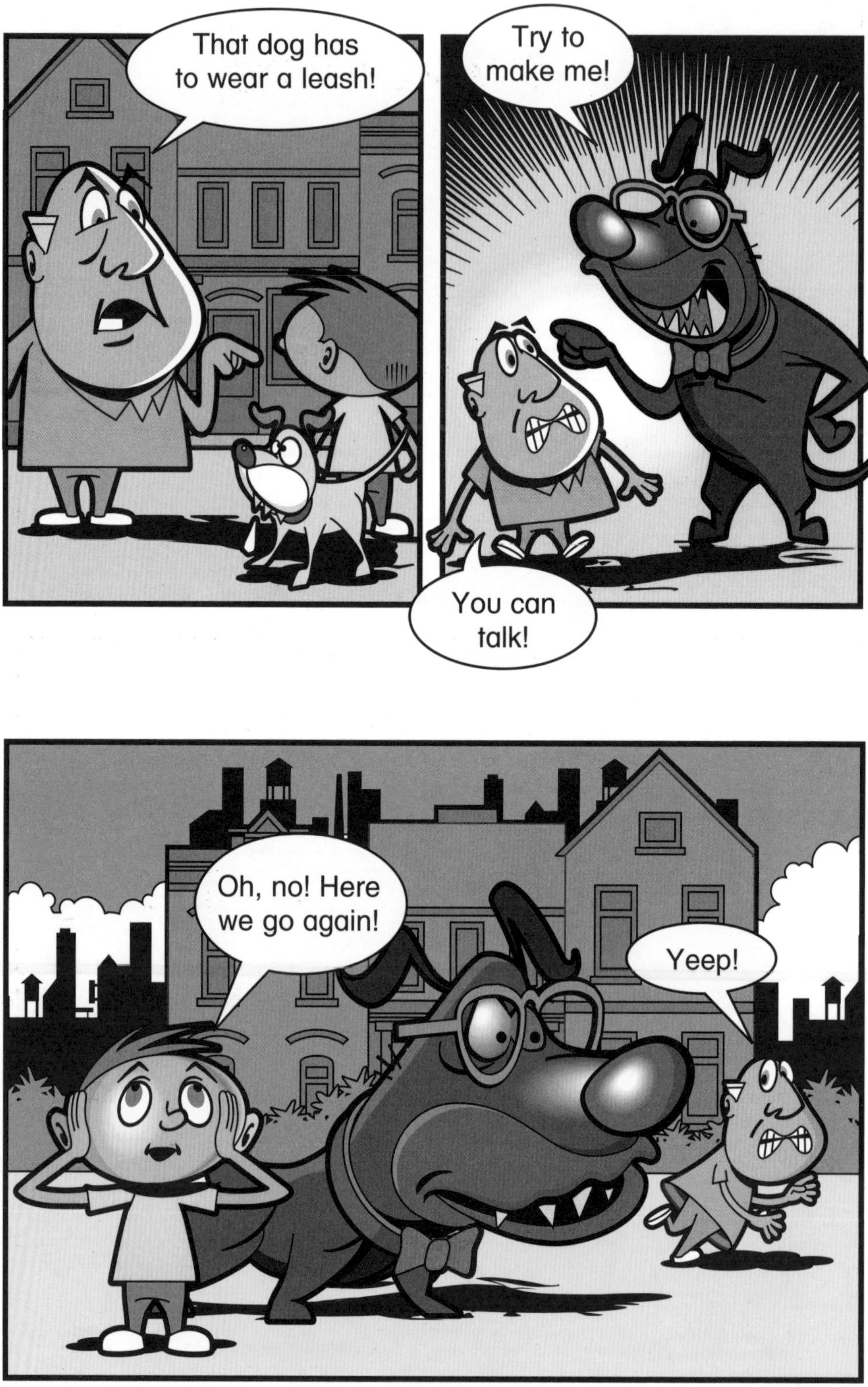
That dog has to wear a leash!
Try to make me!
You can talk!
Oh, no! Here we go again!
Yeep!